Ozzie in Tiddley Winks

by
Mike J.
Preble

This is a
made-up
Story-Time
Bookie
to be read
while eating
a cookie
(or something)

Dedicated to
my
Girl Friend
Ann Marie

This is a story about
OZZIE.
He is the World's
Tiddley Winks
Champion !!

When he was a
little boy, Ozzie
always said he
wanted to be the
very best
Tiddley Winker
in the
World!

Ozzie would practice his Tiddley Winks every day. He practiced when it was Sunny.

Ozzie practiced when it was dark.

(Draw something you practice)

OZZIE even practiced when it was raining.

Draw a picture that has rain in it. (Be creative!)

With all of his
practice at
Winking, Ozzie
became the best
Tiddley Winker
in the World.
He set many World
Records with his
Famous Winking.

The World's

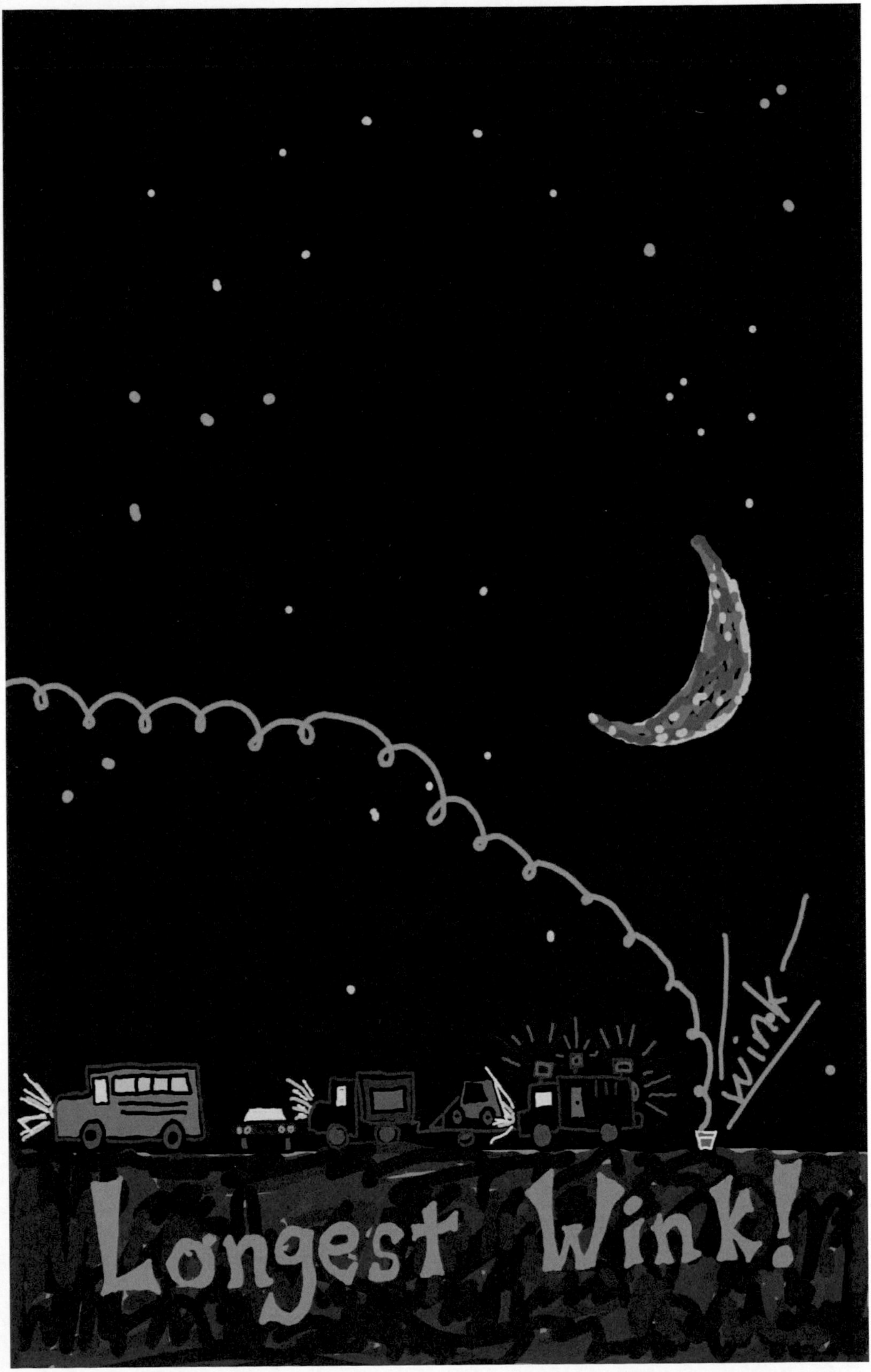
Wink
Longest Wink!

Fastest to 100 Winks!

Most Winks in a row!

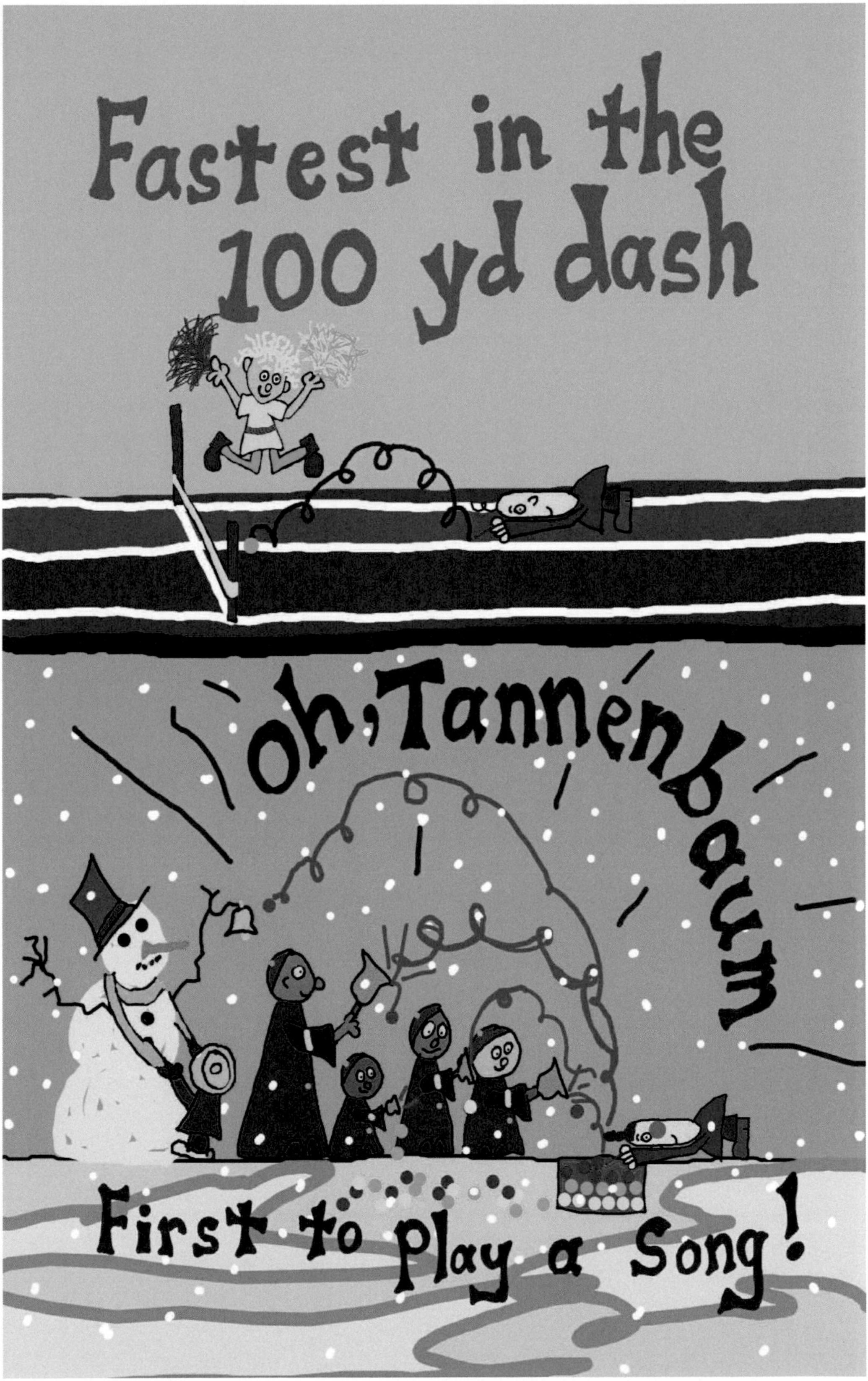
Fastest in the 100 yd dash
oh, Tannenbaum
First to play a Song!

The World's
Biggest
Wink!

He could also do Trick Shots

Draw your own →

Ozzie was the best Winker ever! He tiddled all over the World.

Sir Tommy Tiddle
Earl of Winks

Draw some places you have seen.

Write Something

One day Ozzie went to the local Winkers Club.

Inside he met
Wendie Winkle,
the Women's
World Champion.
Ozzie and Wendy
fell in love.
And they winked
happily ever after.

The End.

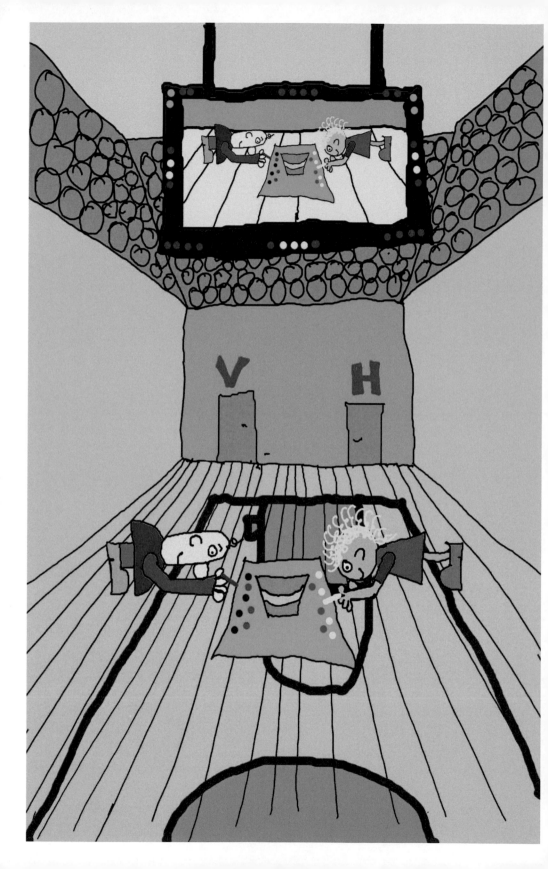